Sandy Lane Stables

Sandy Lane Stables

Horse in Danger

Michelle Bates

Adapted by Caroline Young

Reading consultant: Alison Kelly

Series editor: Lesley Sims

Designed by Brenda Cole

Cover and inside illustrations: Barbara Bongini and Ian McNee

Map illustrations: John Woodcock

This edition first published in 2016 by Usborne Publishing Ltd.,
Usborne House, 83-85 Saffron Hill, London EC1N 8RT, England.
www.usborne.com

Copyright © Usborne Publishing 2016, 2009, 2003, 1997

Illustrations copyright © Usborne Publishing, 2016

The name Usborne and the devices ♀ 🌐 are Trade Marks of
Usborne Publishing Ltd. UKE

A CIP catalogue record for this book is available from the British Library.

Contents

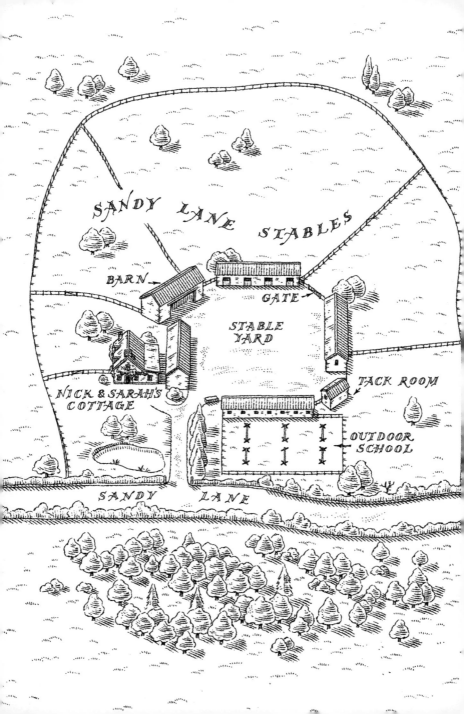

Chapter 1

Breaking Up and Making Up

It was the first day of the autumn half term. Rosie Edwards was usually buzzing with excitement at the prospect of spending a whole, glorious week at Sandy Lane Stables, but this time it was different. Rosie and Jess Adams, her best friend, were not getting on very well, so being at the stables was a lot less fun these days.

At the beginning of the school year, Jess had started going out with a boy in their year, and things just weren't the same any more. She was hardly ever around after school or at the weekends, and whenever the two friends did manage to hang out together, it usually ended in a row. Rosie tried to hide her feelings, but she was really hurt: Jess had always been her closest friend, and she hated the way things were between them now...

Not that Jess was the easiest person to be friends with, Rosie reminded herself. She was bold, stubborn and never wrong, which was exactly what had caused their latest argument. Jess's pony, Skylark, had injured herself but Jess had ignored Rosie's advice and taken Skylark out for a ride, which had left her lame for a week. Rosie had told her what she thought, but this had only made Jess absolutely furious. In fact, they had not spoken since the argument, which was making Rosie more miserable than ever.

It was so tempting not to go to Sandy Lane today and simply stay in bed. But she'd be letting down Nick, the stable owner, if she did that and she wouldn't dream of it. She had to go.

"Morning," her mum said cheerily, when Rosie got downstairs. "Off to Sandy Lane today?"

"Guess so."

"I thought you loved it there. Is something up?" her mother asked. "You've been so grumpy lately."

"No I haven't," said Rosie, grumpily.

"Oh dear, have you quarrelled with Jess again?" her mum asked.

"Why can't you just leave me alone?" Rosie snapped, and then immediately felt guilty. "Oh, I'm sorry, Mum. It's no big deal, really."

"Okay," said her mum. "But you know where I am if you need me."

"Thanks," Rosie said, trying to smile. "Really, I'm fine. I'll see you later."

Pulling her woolly hat down over her ears, Rosie set off for the stables on her rickety old bike. It was a cold October day and the lanes were covered with a thick carpet of fallen leaves. Rosie pedalled as fast as she could to keep warm and was in the stable yard in less than ten minutes, beating her all-time record. The exercise made her feel much better, as it always did.

Across the yard, she saw Tom Buchanan and his horse, Chancey. She hadn't seen him around the stable for weeks and had missed him. He was two years older than Rosie and a star rider, but he never bragged about it.

"Hello Rosie," he called across.

"Hi Tom." She smiled. "Where have you been?"

"Revising," he said. "I have mocks after Christmas and Mum's had me chained to my desk."

"Parents!" said Rosie, with a mock scowl. "I'm sure you'll do brilliantly, though. Any sign of Nick and Sarah?"

"Not yet," Tom answered. "We could make a start on the jobs I guess."

Rosie nodded and began to sweep the yard. She couldn't help sneaking a glance over to Skylark's stable, but there was no sign of Jess. Late again.

"Seen Jess at all?" she asked Tom casually.

"Nope, but Nick's going to be hopping mad if she

keeps on being late like this."

Jess had won Skylark in a competition and Nick had agreed to stable the pony on the understanding that Jess looked after her. The deal was that Jess got the stabling fees at a reduced rate, and Nick used Skylark in lessons. It all worked out pretty well... *if* Jess was around.

Hmm, Rosie thought. Maybe if she groomed Skylark, Nick would be happy and perhaps let Jess off being late. Sliding back Skylark's stable door, Rosie went into the grey Arab's box and patted her.

"And how are you this morning, madam?" she asked. "Did you sleep well?"

Skylark snorted as if to reply and Rosie laughed. "Well, let's get you cleaned up," she said.

But as she was leading Skylark out of the stable, Jess cycled into the yard. "Hi," she said to Tom. Then she noticed Rosie holding Skylark. "Oh, so you're in charge of my pony now, are you?"

Rosie was flabbergasted. "I just thought that if I got Skylark ready it would stop you from getting into trouble again. How was I to know you were going to bother turning up today?"

"And just what's that supposed to mean?"

"Well, you haven't exactly been around much lately, have you?" Rosie bit her tongue to stop herself saying more.

Jess stomped over, grabbed Skylark's headcollar out of Rosie's hands and yanked the pony off across the yard.

Rosie watched them in dismay.

"Don't worry," Tom said, walking over. "She's just in a foul mood today."

"But she's always in a foul mood these days," Rosie said sadly. "And I've made things worse, when I wanted to help her and make them better."

"It's not you, it's that her pride's been dented."

"What do you mean?" Rosie was puzzled.

"Well I heard she'd been dumped by her boyfriend," said Tom.

"Oh no." Rosie felt dreadful for Jess, but also a little hurt that Jess hadn't even bothered to tell her.

They were supposed to be best friends.

Coming to a decision, Rosie walked over to Skylark's stable door, but then hesitated outside. "Jess, are you OK?"

"Go away," Jess said, muffling a sob.

Hearing the sob, Rosie rushed into the box and hugged Jess who started crying in earnest.

"Oh Jess, I'm so sorry," said Rosie. "Tom told me what happened, but, well, you know you still have me and Skylark."

"I know..." Jess sniffed. "*I'm* sorry Rosie, I haven't been a very good friend recently. In fact, I'm not sure why you put up with me."

"Me neither," Rosie said, grinning and offering her a crumpled tissue. "It'll be all right, you know. Come on, let's get tacked up."

Jess gave her a watery grin in return. "I am never going to get so upset over a silly boy ever again. Ever..." she added. "Friends?"

"Yes," said Rosie, with a nod. "Friends."

Chapter 2

Dreadful News

Rosie and Jess didn't stop working all morning, and had only just finished when Alex and his sister, Kate, arrived.

"Are we in time for cross-country training?" Kate called, hurrying straight over to the stables to get Feather tacked up, as Alex headed for Hector.

"Just," Rosie reassured her. "Nice to see you too, Alex," she added, trying not to sound surprised. Kate spent every day of the holidays at the yard, but Alex rarely came these days.

Within a few minutes, the four riders stood

holding their horses in the middle of the yard, waiting for Nick to take them out over the cross-country course.

"Hi you lot," he said, coming out of his cottage. "You're not going to like this, but I'm afraid I can't take you this morning after all. I've just had a call from a new rider who's booked twelve private lessons, and the only free slot I have is now."

They were all disappointed, but stifled their groans. Private lessons made the stables money and Nick couldn't afford to turn down a private client. As much as they loved Sandy Lane, all four of them knew how much it cost to keep the place running.

"I promise I'll take you out as soon as I can," Nick said. "But for now, I'd rather you stuck to a hack. Tom's going to take you out instead."

"Cool," said Rosie, smiling as Tom led Chancey out of his stable. "All the old gang reunited."

"Not quite. Izzy and Charlie aren't here," Jess reminded her.

"Izzy's back tomorrow, isn't she?" asked Rosie.

"Yep. Can't wait," Kate broke in. Izzy was her best friend, and she missed her now that she was away at boarding school.

"So, is Izzy coming on the treasure hunt, Kate?" Jess asked.

"You bet," she answered. "She's my partner."

Nick had organized a treasure hunt ride for the next day and everyone was looking forward to it.

"Does anyone know if Charlie's coming back from racing school for the hunt?" Rosie wondered.

"I think it's too far," said Tom. "Shame though... Right, let's get going."

The string of horses headed off in single file towards Bucknell Woods, and turned down the coastal track that led to the beach. As a fresh, autumn wind blew and the sun shone, Rosie felt happier than she had done for weeks.

The five riders stopped on the cliff top and looked down at the sea churning beneath them, before going down the track and onto the sands. There, Tom signalled for them to canter and they raced along the beach in sheer bliss.

"That was brilliant," Jess whooped, pulling Skylark up beside Chancey.

"Let's head over to the bottom of those cliffs. Then we'll turn round and go back," Tom decided.

As they reached the end of the beach, Tom called out for them to turn and they cantered back along the sand, up the track and across the scrubland, only stopping as they neared the woods. Soon, they were going back up the lane to the stables, chatting and laughing after their exhilarating ride.

In the yard, Nick was talking to a man none of them recognized. They seemed to be having a pretty lively conversation.

"Ah you're back. Come over here a moment," Nick called.

The riders tied up their horses before hurrying over to him.

"These are my regular helpers," Nick said, introducing them to the small, wiry man who stood in front of him. "This is Mr. O'Grady – head lad at the Elmwood Racing Stables – where Charlie trained last summer, remember?"

The four riders nodded.

"Well, he has some shocking news: Silver Dancer has been stolen."

Rosie gasped. Silver Dancer was a famous racehorse – a local celebrity. She'd won the Tatford Handicap, and gone on to win the Malvern Stakes, which had made national news. Charlie had loved her dearly when he'd worked with her.

"She was taken last night," Mr. O'Grady told them. "She's entered for a big race a week on Monday, so we must get her back before then."

"Mr. O'Grady thinks one of the stable lads has taken her," Nick said gravely.

"The stable lad is missing, too. It's too much of a coincidence." Mr. O'Grady snorted. "He's a real slacker. I had to have words with him recently, which he didn't like much, but to take the horse..." He paused and shook his head. "And on top of everything else, our trainer, Josh Wiley, is away on holiday for a week. I thought I'd start by asking at all the local stables, in case anyone's seen her."

But none of the Sandy Lane regulars could help.

"Have you spoken to the police?" Nick asked.

"Not yet," Mr. O'Grady said. "The boy will be in serious trouble if I do. I'm sure he'll come to his senses and bring her back. She's a very special horse. We've had her since she was a yearling."

Rosie tried to imagine how she'd feel if one of the Sandy Lane ponies went missing and couldn't. Why would a stable boy steal a racehorse? What could he possibly want with one?

"Anyway, here's a photo of the lad. His name's Jake Goodman."

Everyone looked at the passport-size photo of a boy with a thin face and a shaved head.

"He looks a bit dodgy. In fact, he's not..." But then Mr. O'Grady stopped himself. An awkward silence followed.

Nick spoke first. "If any of you see Jake, or the horse, you're to come straight to me or call Mr.

O'Grady. I'll leave his mobile number on the tack room noticeboard for you."

"Thanks. I must get to the next stables," Mr. O'Grady said, making for his Land Rover. "Please keep an eye out."

"How awful," said Rosie, as he drove away.

"It's a nasty business," Nick agreed, "and poor Mr. O'Grady holds himself entirely responsible. The boy's only been with them six months and he gave him the job in the first place... Now, everyone take a closer look at this photo."

Nick passed the picture around.

"He doesn't look too friendly," said Rosie.

"But everyone looks like a criminal in their passport photo," Jess pointed out.

"You're dead right there." Rosie grinned. "I look like something out of a horror movie."

"All right, you lot, let's untack those hungry horses and get them to their hay nets before they tear down the yard!" said Nick.

Chapter 3

Horse in Hiding

At just past midnight, a solitary horse picked her way through the woods, gliding between the shadows and the darkness. The boy riding her had chosen this way deliberately: nobody would see them at this time of night. Safely hidden, he allowed himself to relax in the saddle. The warm, swaying body beneath him lulled him half to sleep. It was only when the horse stopped abruptly at a fork in the path that he was jolted awake. Which way should they go now? It was so hard to tell...

Letting the reins slip through his fingers, the boy

swung the horse left and they followed a path through the trees. The scent of pine was strong. The horse's hooves sent wafts through the air as they crushed the carpet of needles that covered the ground. The sound of a car made the horse stop in its tracks. They were nearing a road.

The boy hesitated, quickly checked to the left and right and trotted the horse across the tarmac getting to the other side without being seen.

Calmly, he walked the horse on. The only light came from the full moon above them. The boy kept looking for somewhere to hide for the night but this was isolated countryside.

The horse stopped again when they reached a broken-down gate.

"What's wrong?" the boy asked. "Oh, I get it. End of the road, eh?"

He jumped to the ground and pulled the reins up over the black thoroughbred's head, tying the horse to a fence for a moment. As he heaved the old gate open, he saw a battered sign hanging off it and bent closer until he could just make out two roughly painted words on it: 'South Grange'.

"Hmm, I wonder what's at South Grange," he said aloud as he remounted. "Let's take a look."

The path was long and twisting, with thick rhododendron bushes on both sides. It seemed that they had been walking for ages when a large house loomed up ahead.

It was clear that nobody lived in it. Many of the windows were broken, and some had been boarded up, their painted frames faded, chipped and covered with ivy and creeper.

The boy jumped to the ground and tied the horse to some iron railings, giving her a gentle pat.

"Won't be long," he murmured and made his way round to the back of the house, where overgrown lawns stretched out in front of him. To his left, two grassy paddocks were eerily lit by moonlight. Quickly, he went to the side of the house, finding an old yard and what looked like stables. This had once been home for a lot of horses, the boy could tell.

The first stall he looked in was empty, but the unmistakable smell of hay still lingered. The next one was filled with wooden crates. Then he looked in a stable in the far corner and started to feel better. It was filled with bales of hay. They were a little musty, but they would stop his horse going hungry. Closing the stable door, he saw a water pump in the corner of the yard. The whole set-up was perfect. For the first time since he'd left the stables, the boy felt a spark of hope.

Swiftly, he made his way back to the horse who was impatiently pawing the ground.

"All right, all right Dancer," he said, untying the reins. "Let's get you fed and watered. It seems like we've found ourselves somewhere to stay – at least for tonight."

Chapter 4

Treasure Hunt

The day of the Sandy Lane treasure hunt dawned cloudy but dry. As Rosie cycled into the yard, she saw Izzy in the group of riders.

"Hi Izzy, how are you?" she called across, pleased to see her back.

"Glad to be here." Izzy smiled.

Rosie smiled too as she made her way to get Pepper ready. Soon, she was leading him out to join the others. Izzy was riding Midnight, Tom was riding Chancey and Alex was riding Hector. Kate was on Feather and of course Jess was on Skylark.

Rosie grinned at Jess, her partner on the treasure hunt. "Let's hope we do better than last year. We were hopeless."

"We can't do much worse," said Jess with a groan. "But remember, no helping anyone else."

"Agreed," Rosie said.

"Gather round, everyone." Nick brought the chatting to an end. "Okay, this is a bit different from a normal treasure hunt. There are ten clues which will give you ten secret locations. When you've worked out where they are, you need to ride there and find a coloured marker – either a ribbon or a big piece of paper pinned up. Write down the colour and then go on to the next one. Is that clear?"

Everyone nodded.

"Right, it's eleven o'clock now. The winners are the ones who've got the names of the most places and colours by three. You've got to cover a big area, but no clue is more than a fifteen minute ride away," he added, winking at Kate. She had ridden miles out of her way last year and was still embarrassed.

"I hope that the weather holds out for you," Nick finished, "but rain is forecast, so you'd better get going. Everyone get a sheet of questions from Sarah." He pointed to his wife, who was holding out a sheaf of papers with one hand, while holding their two month old baby, Zoe, on her hip.

All the riders took a sheet, and Rosie flicked through the questions. "Oh no, they're impossible."

"Hey, let's follow those two," Jess hissed, watching Tom and Alex leave the yard and head down the lane. "They're going towards Sandy Lane Cove, so they must know what they're looking for."

"Okay," Rosie said, not so sure. They followed the boys at a safe distance, but by the time they'd reached the cliff tops they had lost sight of them altogether.

Jess drew Skylark to a halt. "Where *are* they?"

"Looking for us?" A grinning Tom appeared from a clump of trees.

"Thought you could just be our hangers-on, did you?" Alex added, cantering past. "Well, we've got the marker already. Byeee!"

"Just wait! We'll beat you," Jess cried. "I'm sure we can get it too," she added to Rosie.

"Of course we can. Tom and Alex came from this path," said Rosie, heading into the trees.

But after twenty minutes of searching, they still hadn't found the marker.

"We're wasting time here," Jess said, crossly. "The answer must be staring us in the face, but we just can't see it. We'll have to come back to this one."

"Yes, we really need to start getting some colours," Rosie agreed.

"Why don't we look at all of the clues again and see if there are any we can answer before we set off?" suggested Jess.

It was starting to drizzle, so the girls huddled under some trees to read the questions. Skylark and Pepper snapped at each other as they stood waiting.

"Stop it you two," said Rosie. "Oh dear, they're as fed up as we are!"

"I don't blame them." Jess laughed. "Look at this clue – 'A watery reserve in the middle of the woods'.

That's got to be the pond in Bucknell Woods."

"Yeah. Let's go," Rosie said, trotting off on Pepper.

Cantering along the grass verge, the girls passed Sandy Lane and rode into the woods. It wasn't long before they reached the pond. The two girls circled their ponies around the left bank, but there wasn't a colour in sight.

"Let's try the other side," said Jess.

"But it'll take ages to ride over there if we take the bridleways." Rosie sighed. "We'd better look though."

They rode off in a glum silence and when they finally reached the other side, there was no marker there either.

"Perhaps it wasn't Bucknell Woods after all," Jess said, her voice miserable. "Could it be the reservoir beyond Mr. Wells' pig farm? There are woods there."

"Jess, it's half twelve already," said Rosie. "I think we should go on to clue three and come back to this one too. 'A place to practise your jumping skills. Look for the wood nearest me.' That's got to be the outdoor school. What about the old oaks at the bottom of Sandy Lane? Shall we try there?"

"Okay," said Jess.

So they cantered off to the end of the lane to look around the trees.

"I was so sure we had this one in the bag," Rosie said, when ten minutes later they'd found nothing.

"How are you doing?" Izzy asked, as she and Kate rode past. "We've got three."

"Three!" Jess wailed. "We haven't got a single one. Tom and Alex led us off to Sandy Cove and we were hanging around there for half an hour."

"Never mind," said Izzy. "There'll be payback, you'll see."

"We've got this one," Kate said, "so I'll give you a clue. You're close but the wood isn't the wood of the tree you're looking at."

"Thanks," Rosie answered and, as she turned to the lines of fir trees at the top of the outdoor school, she saw of a piece of paper stuck to the last one.

"Got it! Yellow!" she shouted to Jess.

But Jess still wasn't happy. "We're so far behind.

Why don't we split up and meet by those trees over there in, say, an hour?"

"I don't know. We're not really supposed to split up." Rosie sounded uncertain.

"Nick will never know," Jess wheedled. "And if we carry on at this rate, we'll be so far behind the others we'll never hear the end of it."

"All right then," Rosie agreed. "I'll take the next three questions."

Jess nodded and waved as she rode off.

Feeling hopeful, Rosie read her first clue aloud. "Take the left-hand path at Sandy Lane Cove, then look for a four-legged home. Well, I bet that's a stable. Let's see what we can find." She turned Pepper and cantered off.

The countryside was pretty deserted, and Rosie saw nobody else for a long time. She'd never ridden this way before and she was getting further and further from Sandy Lane. As she began to get near Walbrook, she found a rusty old gate across the track in front of her. It was half open.

"What's this, eh Pepper?" she muttered, patting her pony. Jumping down, she saw a piece of board on the ground with two words painted on it. "South Grange... Hmm, worth a look, I suppose. There could be a 'four-legged home' here."

Rosie was pretty sure that she'd ridden further than the fifteen minutes Nick had mentioned, but then she saw hoof-prints in the mud. Perhaps she wasn't the first treasure hunter to come this way. Back on Pepper, she followed the prints until a huge house came into view.

Rosie let out a low whistle. "What a house! It looks deserted but I do hope we're not trespassing. Well, they must have some stables here, Pepper. Let's get searching!" she finished brightly, trying to sound confident. The place had an eerie feel and it was starting to make her uncomfortable.

Jumping down, she tied Pepper to a tree and turned the corner of the house, then crossed the yard beyond. Walking over, she looked inside a stable and waited for her eyes to get used to the gloom… Nothing but a pile of crates. Then, she stopped dead. She was certain she could hear a horse snuffling and snickering. The noise was coming from the stable at the far corner of the yard, which had both sections of the door bolted… Rosie suddenly felt very nervous.

She crossed to the stable, pulled back the bolt and slowly opened the door. As she did, hands reached out and grabbed her. She screamed as she was pulled into the dim stable.

"Aagh! Aagh! Someone… HELP!"

"Please, be quiet!" a boy's voice begged in the dark. "You'll upset Dancer."

With a start, Rosie realized that the voice was talking about Silver Dancer, the stolen racehorse. She tried to scream again, but a hand slapped across her mouth and only a muffled wail came out.

"If you'll just keep quiet, I'll let go," the voice promised her.

As Rosie struggled, the door opened a fraction and light flooded in to reveal… the thin-faced boy she'd seen in the black and white photo.

"Please calm down. I'm not going to hurt you."

Rosie hesitated, and the boy took his hand away from her mouth and loosened his grip.

"What are you doing here?" he asked.

"I-I'm on a t-treasure hunt," Rosie stammered.

"Look, I'm really sorry I scared you," the boy said. He looked as nervous as Rosie felt.

Rosie looked behind him and saw a horse – an exquisite black mare. Rosie had never seen a horse quite like her. Her features were so fine, her legs so delicate that they didn't look strong enough to take the weight of the muscled body above them. She was a perfect thoroughbred racehorse.

"She's rather nervy," the boy explained. "There... It's all right girl," he whispered, his voice soft and soothing. Rosie couldn't help admiring his knack with the horse.

"You can't keep me here," she said, trying to sound brave. "I know who you are. Everyone's looking for you, and they'll come looking for me now, too."

"Keep you here?" The boy started to laugh. "What makes you think I'd want to keep you here? I didn't ask you to come looking for us, did I?" He snorted.

"No, but—"

"To be honest, now you have found us, I could really do with some help," the boy interrupted.

"Help you?" Rosie was indignant. "When you've stolen a horse?"

"I know it seems bad, but it's not how it looks," the boy said. "I've taken Dancer for her own good. I can't tell you what's going on, but she was in serious danger, believe me. I'm going to take her back just as soon as Josh gets home."

"As soon as Josh gets home?" Rosie repeated, slowly backing towards the door.

"Oh no you don't." The boy moved across the stable blocking her way.

"I have to go," she insisted, her mouth dry with fear. "My friend's waiting for me."

"You can't," the boy started to say. A worried look flashed across his face. "Please... Not yet."

He sounded tired and desperate. Rosie looked at him more closely. He seemed younger than in his photo – probably only a few years older than her.

"But I've got to meet my friend at a quarter to two," she explained.

The boy hesitated. "I see," he said. "The thing is, I've really messed up and we haven't got enough food. There's some old hay in the other stable, but Dancer needs oats. Do you think you could get some and bring them here tomorrow?"

Rosie decided instantly that if saying 'yes' would get her out of there, she would agree to anything.

"This is to pay for them," the boy said, handing over a ten pound note.

Rosie was surprised. A thief, offering to pay?

"If you won't do it for me, do it for Dancer," he begged. "She needs the right food."

Rosie looked at the beautiful racehorse again. "If I do, you must promise to explain everything."

The boy looked doubtful.

"Otherwise no deal," she said firmly.

"Okay then," he agreed at last. "But you mustn't tell anyone. You can't."

Rosie nodded uncertainly.

"You won't regret this," the boy said. He sounded relieved and grateful. "I'm Jake by the way."

"I know," Rosie answered. "I'm Rosie."

She ran towards Pepper, and quickly rode away. The further they got from South Grange, the more convinced she was that she had to tell Nick about Silver Dancer. Once she had done that, everything was bound to be all right...

Chapter 5

A Guilty Conscience

Rosie didn't stay so sure about telling Nick for long. The boy had trusted her, even given her money – she couldn't turn him in without giving him a chance to explain. And there had been something about him that made her want to believe him. He loved horses, that was clear, so he must have had a good reason for doing what he had done.

Spurring Pepper on, she cantered over to where Jess was waiting for her.

"I've been waiting ages," said Jess, crossly. "What took you so long?"

"Sorry. I, um, went further than I'd thought."

"We've only got an hour and ten minutes left," Jess grumbled. "I got the one about the watery reserve – it *was* over by Mr. Wells' pig farm – blue. And then there was a green ribbon by the garage and orange by the lamp post at the end of Sandy Lane. Oh, and the pink and purple were easy as well," she said, her voice speeding up in excitement as she shuffled through the questions. "They were by the duck pond and the old barn. So that gives us six. How many answers did you get?"

"Sorry, what was that?" Rosie said. She hadn't been listening at all. Her head was full of stolen racehorses and unanswered questions.

"How many colours did you get?" Jess repeated.

"Oh, er, none," Rosie replied.

"You haven't been listening to a word I've been saying, have you?"

"Yes, yes I have," said Rosie. "And I'm sorry, I haven't done as well as you but—" She shrugged.

"Have I done something wrong?" Jess asked.

"You were so up for this treasure hunt earlier..."

"I'm sorry," Rosie said again. "I'm just wet, tired and fed up. Let's go and look for the clue at Sandy Lane Cove, the one we couldn't find before."

"All right," Jess agreed.

But they had no luck this time either.

"Come on. We've got to get back," Jess said at last. "Time's nearly up."

Rosie didn't say anything. She couldn't think about the treasure hunt any more, and wanted only to get back to the yard.

"Hi, how have you done? Got all the answers?" Nick welcomed them back.

"Only six," Jess mumbled.

Nick laughed. "Oh dear. They weren't as difficult as all that, were they?"

Jess shrugged her shoulders. "Guess Rosie and I aren't very good at this sort of thing," she said. Something was up with Rosie, she was certain.

Izzy and Kate came back next.

"We've got all but two of the answers," Izzy cried.

"Better than us then," Jess muttered.

All the other riders started arriving soon afterwards, with Tom and Alex coming in last.

"I make it two minutes past three," Nick said, taking their question sheet. "But seeing as you haven't won anyway, it doesn't really matter."

"We haven't?" Tom looked crestfallen. "All that hard work for nothing. Who's won then?"

"Well, Natalie and Simon have beaten you for starters. They've got nine." Nick grinned.

Tom grinned back. He didn't really mind not winning and even led the cheering as the winners collected their prizes.

"Right, let's get these horses cleaned up, and then we can start on tea," said Nick.

Nick and Sarah had invited everyone to their cottage, which was usually great fun, but Rosie didn't feel like going today.

She stayed with Pepper for as long as she could. When she walked in, the room was packed.

"Come on, Rosie, or we'll miss the food," Jess

cried, pushing her way to the table of sandwiches, pizzas, crisps and cakes.

"Sorry we didn't help you out by Sandy Lane Cove," Tom called across. "We were taking the treasure hunt seriously."

"Well thanks for wasting our time," Jess said. "And you didn't even win." A mischievous grin spread across her face.

Rosie felt as if she were there, but at the same time, not really there at all. The happy chatter of her friends became a loud, humming throb that made it difficult for her to concentrate. She knew that she should tell Nick about the stolen racehorse, but, somehow, she couldn't. It just didn't feel like the right thing to do, not yet.

She woke up very early the next morning and it took her a few moments to remember what was bothering her, and what had given her such disturbing dreams.

When she did remember, she started to panic.

She needed some serious answers. She was dressed, out of the door and on her bike within minutes. If she hurried, she could get to South Grange and back in time for breakfast.

She found the boy, Jake Goodman, in the yard.

"Hey! I didn't expect you this early," he said.

"Look, I haven't been to the fodder merchant yet. I need to know more first."

"Don't you trust me?" he asked. "I guess not. You can't trust anyone these days, can you? I nearly left here yesterday... wasn't sure I trusted you. I thought you might raise the alarm."

Rosie didn't know what to say. He'd never know how close she'd come to doing just that.

"How did you get here?" he asked bluntly. "On your own?"

"Yes, I cycled," Rosie said.

"Well, thanks for coming," he said. "How much do you know already?"

"Only that you've been working at the Elmwood Racing Stables for the past six months and that you've stolen their best horse."

"Ha!" Jake snorted.

"And that the head lad's called in at Sandy Lane," Rosie added.

"O'Grady has?" Jake frowned.

Rosie tried to think back. "Yes... Yes I think that was his name. He wanted to know if any of us had seen you."

"I bet he did." Jake's hands were shaking as he paced up and down the yard. "He'll want to get to me before I can tell Josh everything."

"Look, I don't understand. Please, just explain what's going on," said Rosie.

"It's not that easy!" Jake snapped. "It's just..." he spoke more quietly, "... I'm not sure where to start." He took a deep breath. "Best to keep it simple. O'Grady was planning to nobble Dancer. He was going to ruin her chances in the next big race."

"What?" Rosie said.

"Nobbling, you know doping, drugging... all the same really. I've known something was up for some time now – men used to appear at the yard whenever Josh wasn't around but when I asked O'Grady about them, he told me to mind my own business. So I did – at first. It's always been my dream to work with horses and I didn't want to lose my job. But then Josh went away and I overheard O'Grady on the phone. He was talking about Silver Dancer and planning to dope her, put some stuff in her food." Jake paused for breath. "And a couple of days later, I heard him putting a bet on another horse in her race and that confirmed it for me. You see, Dancer's the clear favourite for the race."

Rosie didn't know what to say.

"I had no choice. I had to get her out of the yard before it was too late," Jake went on. "I took her straightaway – that night. I guess when O'Grady found both of us missing, he put two and two together. So that's the story." He paused again. "You don't believe me, do you?"

"It's not that," Rosie said. "And, in fact, it was a bit strange that O'Grady didn't want to tell the police. But why on earth would he want to spoil Silver Dancer's chances of winning?"

"It's amazing what people will do if you pay them enough," Jake answered sadly. "I don't know who *is* paying him, but it will be a lot of money."

"Haven't you got a phone number for Josh?" asked Rosie. "So you can speak to him directly?"

"I haven't got his mobile number," Jake answered. "Only O'Grady has that."

"Look, there's someone I think might help you," Rosie went on. "I ride at this local stables and the owner, Nick—"

"No way," Jake interrupted sharply.

"But Nick will understand..."

"No," Jake said fiercely. "I'm not involving anyone else in this."

"Well, what are you going to do then?" Rosie snapped. "You can't take her back to the stables and you can't stay here."

Jake looked uncomfortable. "Okay, so I hadn't thought it through very well," he said. "I just panicked, took her and ran. But now that we're here I was thinking I could use this place as a base and stay hidden till Josh gets back. There's a stable for Dancer, great fields for her to train in. I even brought a blanket for her. And there's the water pump too. If you could just bring some oats, then..."

Rosie still wasn't sure if she should trust him, but he had clearly risked everything for this horse. What else could she do but help?

"Okay, I'll bring you some food for Silver Dancer. When does Josh get back?"

"Not till Saturday," Jake answered. "And her race is the Monday after."

"Can you really keep her hidden for a week?"

"I hope so," Jake said. "I've got to... and Josh has *got* to believe me."

His face was pale, and he looked exhausted.

"If you tell him the story, the way you've told it to me, I think he'll believe you," Rosie said. "He's pretty fair, from what Charlie said."

"Was that Charlie Marshall, the boy who did

work experience for us in the summer?" Jake asked.

"Yeah, do you know him?" Rosie looked surprised. "He's a friend of mine."

"Not well, but he was a nice guy," Jake went on. "He had an accident, didn't he?"

"Yes, yes he did," Rosie answered. "And Josh helped sort out a retraining programme for him."

Jake nodded. "That's right. I remember now. Josh is good like that."

"Right, I must go. My parents don't even know I'm out. I've got to be at my stables from eleven to one, but I'll come after that with the food for Silver Dancer. You must be starving, too."

"Her food is more important than mine, but yes I am pretty hungry, to be honest," Jake said. "And I don't suppose there's any chance you could lend me a jumper, could you? Sorry to be cheeky, but it's freezing in here at night."

"I'll see what I can do."

"Thanks a million, Rosie." Jake smiled.

As she left the stall, Rosie turned back to look at

the racehorse as she went. "You're lucky to have someone who cares this much about you," she said to Silver Dancer.

"Beautiful, isn't she?" Jake said, proudly. "But remember you can't tell anyone else about her – or me. Promise?"

"I promise," Rosie replied.

Without another word, she ran to her bike and cycled off down the drive.

Chapter 6

The Lying Starts

"Morning Rosie, you're up early, love." Rosie felt a pang of guilt as her mum bustled around the kitchen making breakfast. Keeping Jake and Silver Dancer a secret from everyone was not going to be easy and she hated not being honest.

"I, um, wanted to make a start on my homework," Rosie said, looking at the table.

"Good for you," her mum said. "It's your first cross-country session this morning too, isn't it? I'll give you a lift to the stables."

"Thanks, but I'll cycle," Rosie said, quickly. She

needed her bike to get to South Grange later.

"I've got to go that way anyway and you don't want to risk being late," her mum insisted.

Rosie sighed. Why did Mum have to be so helpful today of all days? She would have to come back for her bike later, so as not to arouse any suspicions, but that would take time...

The stables were busy for a Monday morning and Rosie could tell straight away that it was going to be tricky for her to slip out to see Jake unnoticed.

"Earth to Rosie." Izzy was staring at her, but she hadn't even noticed.

"Sorry Izzy, I was, er... thinking about the cross-country training session."

"Exciting, isn't it?" Izzy said. "Our first go over the course this year. And the Roxburgh Team Chase isn't that far away now."

"Yeah, you're right," said Rosie, her mind turning to another niggling worry. Cross-country had always been her favourite discipline, but recently she'd noticed that Pepper didn't seem to have the same stamina any more. There was a chance that the little horse wouldn't be chosen to make the team.

"Give us a hand with Midnight's girth, could you – if you're not too busy, that is?" Izzy winked. "I can hardly do it up, he's blowing out so much!"

"Sure, yes, sorry," Rosie replied. She had to try and pull herself together in case anyone guessed that something was up.

"Everyone ready?" Nick called, walking over and joining the group. "We'll be doing daily cross-country sessions from now on, so you need to be here every day if you want to try out for the team. I'll announce who I've picked on Thursday."

Rosie looked around. Jess was here with Skylark, Kate was on Feather and Izzy was riding Midnight. Tom was on Chancey and she was on Pepper – everyone on their favourite mounts. It was going to be tough this year.

"We'll be all right, won't we boy?" Rosie said, leaning down to stroke Pepper's dear, scraggy neck. The pony snorted his answer and broke into a steady trot, which cheered Rosie up enormously.

Nick gathered the riders around him. "Now, I know you all know this course well, but this is our first outing this season and the ground's pretty slippery. We're going to limber the horses up a bit and then I'll send you off at five minute intervals. Concentrate on getting round safely, please. Speed can come later. Is that absolutely clear?"

"Yes, Nick," everyone answered in unison.

"Tom, you go first," he went on. "Jess can follow you and then Rosie."

Rosie nodded.

"Izzy next and Kate can bring up the rear," Nick continued. "I'm going to be at the top of the hill, so don't go too fast – I'll be watching you!"

Rosie smiled as Tom and Chancey flew neatly over the tiger trap.

"Take it easy everyone. Remember, it's just a practice," Nick called out.

Rosie waited for Jess to get a bit ahead and then it was her turn. The jumps were not high, but

Pepper would know about it if he didn't clear them well. They managed the tiger trap easily, galloped over the field and then took the brush hurdle. So far, so good. As they headed into the trees, Rosie started to relax and enjoy herself. She kicked Pepper on to the log pile, and they cantered through the trees, mud spraying up from Pepper's hooves and splattering behind them. Over the tyres they went, then a long hard gallop to the water.

Pepper's sides were heaving, and Rosie knew she was pushing him hard. She took her time over the zigzag rails and cantered up the hill to take the stone wall. As Pepper cleared the last fence, he slowed to a trot and they drew to a halt beside Nick.

"Wow, that was great!" she said. Pepper had gone really well, and Rosie felt her confidence in her horse return as they watched the others finish.

Soon, five steaming horses and riders stood around, waiting for Nick's verdict.

"Not bad," he said. "I'm glad to see that most of you took my advice and went nice and easy. I think we'll get a good team together."

As the riders made their way to the yard, Rosie rode up alongside Jess. "Everyone rode pretty well, didn't they?"

"Oh Rosie, you're not worried, are you?" Jess asked. "You'll get on the team. You always do."

Rosie shrugged. "Izzy and Midnight are really good and Kate's come on a lot, too. And then there's Pepper," she added, quietly.

"What's wrong with Pepper?"

"It's probably nothing," Rosie said, "but he seems to have lost his spirit a bit lately."

"Pepper won't let you down," Jess reassured her.

Rosie smiled, hoping Jess was right. She started to clean Pepper as fast as she could, planning to get away quickly.

"Coming for lunch?" Jess called, waving her lunch box. Rosie had to agree or she'd make Jess suspicious. It was three o'clock before she could head home for her bike.

Rosie waited for the bus in a panic. If only her

mum had let her bring her bike this morning. At last, the bus trundled around the corner, but it seemed to take ages to reach her stop. She let herself into the house, hoping that nobody would hear her. No such luck.

"You're home early," her mum said.

"I came back to collect my *Pony Weekly*," Rosie said, thinking quickly and ashamed she could lie so easily. "I, er, promised to lend it to Jess."

"I don't know," said her mum, disappearing into the utility room. "You're always running around after that girl."

Rosie raced upstairs, grabbing her backpack and rummaging in a bag of clothes that had been ready to go to the charity shop for weeks. She stuffed a couple of her Dad's old jumpers into the backpack and tore back downstairs. Now, food for Jake. An apple, a couple of slices of bread, some cheese and some slices of ham... that would do.

"I'm off," she yelled, remembering to grab her unnecessary *Pony Weekly*. She slammed the door before her mum had time to ask when she'd be back.

Rosie pedalled as quickly as she could. It would be dark soon and she had to hurry. She stopped off at the fodder merchant, but it was difficult to keep her balance on the bike after she had stuffed the heavy oats into her backpack, too.

Racing to the end of the drive of South Grange, she jumped off her bike and rushed into the yard. Her heart sank. The door to the corner stable was wide open.

"Jake?" There was no answer. "Jake... Are you there?" Nothing.

Her mind raced. What if Jake and Silver Dancer had been found by O'Grady? Or perhaps Jake had given up waiting, and fled? She wouldn't have blamed him. She was about to go when she heard a whinny. Peering at the brow of the hill opposite, she could just make out a horse and rider in the twilight.

Jake was hunched tight into a ball on Silver Dancer's back. He looked so perfect, crouched over her with his arms rocking gently backwards and forwards as he fed her the reins. Silver Dancer was straining at the bit, waiting for the slightest release on the reins to go faster, but Jake was in complete control of her. The muscles in her shoulders were taut as she flew across the turf. Rosie was spellbound.

She decided to wait for them in the stables. Soon, she heard the steady clip clop of hooves and the sound of Jake's voice.

"Easy Dancer, that's enough for now. I won't push you too hard tonight. I know it's hard for you, girl... it is for me too," he said, softly. "I'm pretty scared, you know. And we have to be so careful. I dread to think what will happen to me if we get caught."

Rosie smiled at the gentleness in his voice. This boy loved Silver Dancer, it was clear... But she felt embarrassed that she'd heard his private thoughts. She'd been about to go over to them, but now she didn't think she could. She'd see them tomorrow.

Leaving the oats, food and jumpers on a chair in the stable, Rosie crept out. She left them to their supper in peace and cycled home.

Chapter 7

A Friendship Grows

Rosie returned to South Grange early the next morning with more food for Jake. It meant she had to miss the cross-country training session – and she had pretended to Jess that she was helping her mum, which made her feel even guiltier.

Jake was already grooming Silver Dancer as she arrived. "Hi," he said. "Thanks for the food you left."

"You're welcome," said Rosie. "You got the clothes I see," she added, grinning at the sight of Jake in one of her dad's old jumpers.

"Yeah, thanks. I needed them. It's so cold at

night," Jake answered, with a smile.

"Sorry I didn't hang around yesterday," Rosie went on. "I didn't have much time." She didn't want him to suspect that she'd overheard him.

"No worries," Jake said. "I guessed you were busy. O'Grady hasn't been round again, has he?"

"No, I think he's probably looking further afield now, having tried all the local stables."

"That's what I'm hoping, but you will tell me if he turns up again, won't you?" Jake said, nervously.

"Sure thing," Rosie promised.

"Thanks," he said, putting the saddle onto Silver Dancer's back and fastening the girth. "So what's going on at your stables?"

"Well..." Rosie hesitated. "There are a lot of team chases and trials coming up and Nick's about to pick a team. It's normally great, but I'm a bit worried that I won't get picked this year. Lots of other people are good riders, too."

"Feeling stressed, then?"

"A bit, yeah," said Rosie.

"You should use it, let it make you even more determined to succeed. That's what I do. You could try out Dancer today if you like, get some real speed. I bet you're dying to."

"She's too valuable. I couldn't," Rosie spluttered.

"You'll be OK," Jake said. "I'm not suggesting you go galloping off into the distance. Just take her round nice and easy."

Rosie still wasn't sure, but Jake was right. She was desperate to have a go.

"Come on." Jake laughed. "I'll give you a leg-up."

Grabbing her riding hat, Rosie jumped up onto the black horse. Silver Dancer was high – about seventeen hands – and her slim sides felt very different to Pepper's round belly. In fact, it felt really weird sitting up there. The racing saddle was different – more lightweight – and the stirrups were shorter, too.

It was such a shame, Rosie thought, that she could never, ever tell anyone that she had actually ridden a racehorse.

Giving a squeeze with her calves, she moved Silver Dancer forward into an easy trot.

"Take her around the paddock," Jake suggested. "I'll follow on behind."

Rosie patted the downy neck of the black racehorse. "I can't believe how calm she is."

"You should see her on the racecourse – she's so sure of herself. She never gets stressed out. She takes it all in her stride."

Rosie could hear the love and pride in Jake's voice. She could hardly feel the horse beneath her as they glided around the paddock. It was as though they were riding on air. She longed to go faster and try Silver Dancer at a canter.

"OK, bring her over here now," Jake said at last.

Rosie pulled the horse up alongside the fence and jumped to the ground.

"Quite a natural." Jake grinned.

Rosie blushed. She'd been trying her best, but she was sure she must have looked wooden.

As Jake took Dancer around the paddock, Rosie

admired his skill and grace as a rider. Would she ever ride like that? Horse and rider were so perfectly at ease with each other. It was a joy to see.

"We'd better take a break now," he said. "Dancer might lose patience if I take her round that paddock again. Did you bring any food? I'm starving."

"Sure," Rosie said, feeling rather hungry herself. Luckily, she had brought enough for two.

"Thanks, Rosie. I'll feed Dancer first, and then we can eat."

As they tucked into the food Rosie had brought from home, they chatted easily. Jake told Rosie all about his family and she told him about hers. Both were the eldest child and found, to their surprise, that they had a lot in common.

Swallowing his last mouthful, Jake sprang up. "Shall we take Dancer for a hack in the woods? We can take turns."

"I'd love to," Rosie said. With the whole afternoon ahead of them, she realized that there was nowhere she would rather be, not even Sandy Lane.

Chapter 8

Cause for Alarm

The next morning, Rosie cycled to the stables faster than ever. It was nearly eleven and she was going to be late for cross-country. She'd had to go to the fodder merchant for oats and then take them out to South Grange that morning already. Somehow the time had just flown.

As she skidded into the yard, Jess strode towards her. "Cutting it fine, aren't we?"

"I had a bit of a lie-in," said Rosie.

"All right for some." Jess laughed. "Where did you get to yesterday, anyway? You were a bit vague on the phone about what you were up to."

"Oh... Mum needed me. You know how it is."

"Well, you missed a really good session. Tom was there, and Alex and Kate, oh and Izzy too. Midnight was going like a dream."

Rosie suddenly felt hurt. Jess didn't even seem to care that she hadn't been there. "So it was good then, was it?" she asked.

"Brilliant," Jess said. "Nick asked where you were but I told him you had something more important to do. Hey, I know what I meant to tell you – that chap phoned – you know, the one with the missing racehorse. He was in a real panic. His trainer's due back and there's still no sign of the horse, though he had thought he'd got a lead on the boy. He thought someone had seen them..."

"*Someone had seen them*?" echoed Rosie, panic in her voice.

"It turned out to be a retired racehorse on the other side of Ash Hill. It didn't even look like Silver Dancer. He was phoning for news."

"He hasn't given up on finding them locally then?" Rosie asked.

"I shouldn't think you ever give up looking for a horse as valuable as that. I wonder what will happen to that boy when they eventually get their hands on him. He's put them all through so much."

"We don't really know the whole story though, do we?" Rosie snapped, making Jess stare at her. "There's always more to it than meets the eye."

"What do you mean?"

"I just can't believe that someone would be capable of doing something as bad as stealing a horse without a very good reason."

"That's typical of you," said Jess. "Always looking for the good in people. I don't think everyone's as honest as you are, though."

Rosie was embarrassed. She was far from honest these days. She was lying to everyone. "We'd better get ready for cross-country," she said, quickly.

She'd almost given Jake's secret away by panicking. She'd have to be more careful in future, not just with what she said but who she said it to.

"Morning," Tom called across, but Rosie was lost in her thoughts.

She didn't hear a word of Nick's pep-talk before the cross-country course. She couldn't think of anything except Jake, and how scared he would be to hear O'Grady was still looking for him locally.

Rosie was due to go third, but Nick had to call her name twice before she heard him and kicked Pepper into a canter. Nick was timing them, so it was important she was fast today. The little pony cantered to the tiger trap, but then nearly lost his footing and slipped and slid in the mud. Rosie could have kicked herself. It wasn't good to do that right in front of Nick. Pepper was anxious, and they skimmed the top of the brush hurdle as well.

"Concentrate," she muttered to herself, digging her heels deeper into Pepper's sides as he strained towards the log pile. They cleared it, but Pepper had completely lost his rhythm. He checked himself just before the water jump, and Rosie almost flew over his head and into the water. It had been a terrible round. She couldn't bear to watch the other riders come in, not even Jess. She just wanted to get back to the yard.

"I'm off, Rosie," Jess called across.

"Off where?" Rosie was puzzled.

"Shopping with Mum." Jess groaned. "Izzy said she'd sort out Skylark for me."

Rosie was surprised. Jess normally spent all of the holidays at the stables. Her going might mean that Rosie could get to see Jake that day after all. She had assumed she wouldn't be able to slip away unnoticed. Jess had eagle eyes.

"Don't forget, Nick's picking the team tomorrow," Jess called out. "I've arranged to meet Tom and Izzy at half nine. We're going to the beach before the training. Want to join us?"

"Could we make it ten?" Rosie asked, knowing that she'd need time to get to Jake in the morning. "I've got some stuff to do first."

"I'm not sure I can change the arrangements

with Tom and Izzy. Look, I'll wait for you and we can catch them up together," Jess offered, waving goodbye as she hurried out of the yard.

Rosie headed for South Grange as soon as she could but, again, there was no sign of Jake and Silver Dancer in the yard, or in the fields beyond.

"Where can they be this time?" Rosie said to herself. After half an hour of searching and calling, she realized it was pointless. She would come back tomorrow and hope they were all right, but she cycled away with a feeling of foreboding.

When Rosie arrived in the yard the next morning, she found Jake straight away, out in one of the paddocks, cantering a neat circuit around the outside of the school. They were still here, thank goodness. The moment she saw them both, her anxiety vanished. She waved at them happily, and jumped up onto the gate to watch. Jake cantered over to her and drew to a halt.

"Hi there. I didn't expect to see you today."

"I came yesterday afternoon too, but you weren't

around," Rosie said.

"I took Dancer for a ride," he answered.

Rosie shrugged. "Well, I don't want to worry you, Jake, but O'Grady's been phoning around again. Someone thought they'd seen you."

"They did?" There was real fear in Jake's eyes.

"It turned out to be a retired racehorse, but he hasn't given up on finding you locally, apparently, which is a bit worrying."

"I need to be more careful," Jake muttered. "But I've only got to stay hidden for a few more days." He offered the reins to Rosie. "Want a ride?"

"A quick one." Rosie took the reins eagerly. Walking Silver Dancer around the paddock, Rosie looked across to Jake for permission to go a little faster. When he nodded, she squeezed the horse's sides and went straight into an easy canter. She sat deep into the seat, lost in the rhythm of her riding, barely feeling Silver Dancer's hooves touch the ground. It was wonderful.

Drawing up next to Jake, she handed him the

reins and was jumping down as she remembered:

"Oh no!" she exclaimed. "How could I have been so stupid? How could I have forgotten?"

"What? What is it? What have you forgotten?" Jake asked.

"Oh nothing," Rosie muttered. "It's just that I said I'd meet Jess at ten and it's half past already. She's going to be furious with me. I'm going to be late for cross-country training too. I really am losing the plot these days."

As she pedalled crazily along the lanes, Rosie wondered how long she could keep juggling everything without the cracks beginning to show.

Chapter 9

Near Misses

Jess stood in the yard at Sandy Lane and checked her phone. Almost eleven o'clock. Where on earth was Rosie? She stared down the driveway, willing her bike to come round the corner. This lateness was getting ridiculous.

"Coming for the cross-country training, Jess?" Nick asked.

"I said I'd meet Rosie first," Jess answered. "Do you mind if we join the group when she gets here?"

"That's fine. It's not like her to be late though," said Nick. "I hope there's nothing wrong. She left here before lunch yesterday too..."

"I think she's got a lot on," Jess said, though she had no idea what. She was intrigued to learn that Rosie hadn't stayed at Sandy Lane yesterday. What was she up to?

The riders made their way out of the back gate, leaving Jess behind. She thought back over all the times Rosie hadn't been at the yard that week: it wasn't like Rosie at all. Perhaps it was something bad, something serious. Was she ill and hadn't liked to tell Jess? She tried to ring her, but Rosie's mobile was off, so she decided to call her mum instead. She had to know.

As the phone rang in the Edwards' house, Jess half-hoped that Rosie, rather than her mum, would pick up. She had a sneaking suspicion that Mrs. Edwards didn't approve of her.

"Hello, Colcott 626234."

Jess's heart sank. "Hello, er, Mrs. Edwards. It's Jess here, at the stables. Is Rosie about?"

"Rosie?" Mrs. Edwards sounded surprised. "Isn't

she at Sandy Lane with you? She left hours ago."

"Oh." Jess didn't know what to say. She didn't want to get Rosie into trouble. "I've only just turned up, so she's probably on the beach hack," she said. "Sorry to bother you. Bye for now." She ended the call and frowned.

"What's up, Jess?" Tom said. "You look worried."

"Oh nothing, except that I'm waiting for Rosie – again." Jess sighed.

"Well, it looks as though she's forgotten you." Tom grinned.

"Ha ha," Jess replied, sitting on the edge of the water trough to wait.

Rosie finally cycled up the lane at five past eleven. She knew that she'd never be able to tack up and get to training in time, but at least Jess would be out on the cross-country course with the others, she told herself. Except that Jess wasn't. She was standing, with her arms folded, waiting for Rosie and looking very cross indeed.

"Jess, I-I-" she stammered.

"Where have you been this time?"

"Oh... I was helping Mum again," Rosie lied. "And I'm afraid I completely lost track of the time."

"Is that right?"

"Yes. Why?"

"I called your mum five minutes ago and she said you'd left home hours earlier."

"You've been checking up on me, Jess? Really? I'm only five minutes late."

"For cross-country maybe, but you're an hour late to meet me," Jess said. "And I've missed cross-country training because of you, too."

"You shouldn't have waited, then," Rosie snapped. "I'm not answerable to you, anyway. I'd better call Mum and tell her I'm OK. She'll be worried now."

"I covered up for you, told your mum you were probably on the beach hack. Don't ask me why I did, mind you," said Jess, clearly hurt.

"Oh, well thanks," Rosie said, guiltily. "Look, I'm sorry I shouted and I'm really sorry I was so late."

"That's OK," Jess said. "There... there isn't

anything wrong is there? I mean, I've hardly seen you lately and something's up. I'm your best friend. You can tell me anything."

"Nothing's wrong," Rosie said, too quickly.

"You're just being so secretive," Jess went on. "No one ever seems to know where you are. And I thought we'd sorted things out between us, Rosie."

"We have," said Rosie wearily. "And there isn't anything wrong. It's just that I've had a lot on my mind lately, with, er, assignments and stuff."

"Great, if that's all..." Jess said, still unconvinced.

Rosie suddenly felt desperate to tell her friend everything... but she couldn't. Jake could get into such terrible trouble if she did. And she'd promised. "Really, there's nothing," said Rosie, biting her lip.

"Okay," Jess said, uncertainly. "Well, let's tidy up a bit here. Nick said he'd announce the cross-country team today, so we'd better hang around."

"Okay," Rosie said, linking arms as they crossed the yard. She felt very relieved that Jess had decided to let things drop.

Chapter 10

Shocks in Store

Rosie was totally fed up with lying. Her mother had confronted her about the missing food she'd taken for Jake, which meant more lies, and she was still raw about having had to lie to Jess as to why she had been away from Sandy Lane so much lately. When she told Jake how she felt, he was worried too and suggested she stay away from South Grange until Josh was back in two days' time.

Although Rosie knew he was right, she'd felt really low ever since he'd said it. He promised to let her know how things turned out, but she had secretly hoped to stay a part of things and she'd been so sure Jake would need her to back him up with Josh. Now that she thought about it, she realized how foolish she'd been.

"Never mind eh, Pepper?" she said, blowing gently into the piebald's nostrils. "Cross-country for us today. That should cheer us up."

"Morning, Rosie." Nick was striding towards her. "I'm glad I've caught you on your own. I need to talk to you."

"Oh," Rosie said. She suddenly had a horrible feeling that she knew what Nick wanted to talk about and she didn't want to hear it.

"Sound little pony, isn't he?" Nick said, nodding at Pepper.

"Sure is," said Rosie proudly.

"Look, this isn't easy, Rosie, so I'm going to come straight to the point," Nick started. "It's about the cross-country team."

"What about it?" Rosie said, her heart pounding.

"I was going to announce who I'd chosen

yesterday, but I put it off, because I wanted to speak to you alone first. I'm sorry, Rosie, but I'm afraid you're not going to make the team this year. I've chosen Tom, Jess, Izzy and Kate."

Rosie felt a huge lump forming in her throat. She didn't even try to speak.

"Your heart just doesn't seem to be in your riding at the moment," Nick went on.

Rosie nodded. He was right. She had missed a couple of daily practices as well... but to be left out of the team? That was awful.

Just give me another chance, she wanted to shout out, but she couldn't. That would mean telling Nick about Jake, to explain why she hadn't been focused on her riding. She couldn't risk it. Besides, it was too late. Nick had already decided. Tears pricked her eyes, but she tried to hide them.

"I hope you understand," Nick said, patting her shoulder gently. "I'm sure you'll get your place back soon. This is just for the Roxburgh Team Chase, remember, and I'll be reviewing the team after that." He paused, and cleared his throat. "There's just one more thing, Rosie. I know that Pepper's your usual mount, but I'd like Kate to ride him at Roxburgh. He's an experienced little pony and I need one solid score I can count on."

"Oh... No, of course I don't mind," said Rosie, quietly. How could she? Pepper wasn't her pony to say who could and couldn't ride him. She almost laughed at herself. There she had been worrying that Pepper was losing his pace, when Nick saw her as the real problem, not Pepper at all.

"There's cross-country training at eleven," Nick said. "Coming with us?"

"I think I'd rather be on my own for a bit," Rosie replied, trying to smile.

"OK," Nick said kindly. "Chin up."

Nick strode off in the direction of the tack room and Rosie felt the bitterness of her disappointment spreading through her. She wanted to howl and wail. Nick had been nice about it, but she was still devastated, and she certainly couldn't face the others. The only person who would understand was Jake, though he had told her to stay away. But he'd understand when she told him. It was starting to rain so she grabbed her waterproof jacket from the tack room and set off on her bike.

Rosie pedalled as fast as she could. By now, it was pouring, and although the rain washed the tears off her face, it was still pretty difficult to see clearly. As she whizzed down the lane, a car swerved to avoid her, narrowly missing another cyclist on her way to the stables: Jess.

Jess stopped and blinked the rainwater out of her eyes, watching the hunched figure on the bike disappear down the lane.

"That was Rosie," she muttered. "Where's she off to at a quarter to eleven? We're supposed to be going out over the cross-country course this morning."

Jess knew for certain now that something was very wrong. She knew too that she had to follow her friend and find out once and for all exactly what was going on.

Staying out of sight, she followed Rosie for miles, through lanes and past the woods and, finally, up a muddy driveway which led to a large ruined house. When Rosie disappeared around a corner, Jess parked her bike, crept after her... and then stopped, ducking behind a tree. She could hear voices.

In front of her, she could make out a yard, a black horse and Rosie, who was crying. There was another person there, too – a boy? Whoever he was, he had clearly upset her friend.

At that moment, the boy turned around. Jess gasped. It was the boy from the photo – the one who'd stolen the racehorse! What was he doing here and why was Rosie with him? Did she want to be here, or did he have some hold over her? A shiver ran down Jess's spine. This didn't look good.

Jess set off back to Sandy Lane as fast as she could. She would tell Nick, and he could tell O'Grady that she had found his horse and the runaway stable boy. That was the best way to help them all, she was sure.

Chapter 11

A Grave Mistake

Rosie sniffed and blew her nose. "I'm sorry to have bothered you, Jake. I just needed to talk to someone. I know it's the last thing you need, especially when you've got to face Josh tomorrow."

"Don't worry. I understand and I'm glad you came. I'm really grateful for your help, Rosie." His voice was kind but he looked worried.

Rosie could understand why. There was so much at stake for him and no guarantee that Josh would believe his story. "Have you decided how you're going to do this?"

"Josh is back tomorrow. I'm going to see him first thing. If I get to his house early, O'Grady won't be around. And then it's up to me to convince him."

"Well, look, I'd better head off but... good luck," said Rosie, warmly.

"Thanks." Jake grinned. "You too. I'm sure you'll get your place back, you know. You're too good a rider not to."

With a wave over her shoulder, and feeling a lot better, Rosie cycled out of the yard.

Jess had returned to Sandy Lane to find the yard empty. The cross-country ride wouldn't be back for twenty minutes. She couldn't wait for Nick, she decided. This was too important. She would phone Elmwood Racing Stables herself.

Jess found the number easily on the board in the tack room and called it. A gruff voice answered.

"Elmwood Racing Stables."

"Hello, could I speak to Mr. O'Grady?" Jess said.

"Speaking. Who is this?"

Jess gulped. "I... Well, you don't know me," she began, her boldness fading quickly. "I'm Jess Adams and I've got some information for you about your missing racehorse."

"This had better not be a crank call," the man said. "Have you seen her?"

"Well, I think I have," Jess said. "She's with that Jake Goodman and I know where they are. My friend was with them and she was crying..."

"I'm not interested in that nonsense. WHERE ARE THEY?" he bellowed.

"They're at a deserted old house, South Grange. It's over near Walbrook," Jess blurted out, shocked at O'Grady's rudeness.

"Well, you can tell your friend from me she's in big trouble too," he spat, slamming down the phone.

Jess felt sick. O'Grady had seemed all right when he had visited the yard, but just now he had sounded really menacing. Jess was beginning to wonder exactly what she had done, and whether she had only made things worse, when Rosie appeared.

"Are you okay, Jess?" Rosie called cheerily. "You look terrible. Look, if you're worried about the cross-country team, don't be. I'm cool about it."

"It's not that," said Jess quietly.

"Don't feel sorry for me," Rosie went on. "I know I haven't been riding well lately..."

"Rosie, it's not the team." Jess tried again.

"I'm just glad you got in and I'll get my place—"

"ROSIE!" Jess shouted. "Would you please listen to me for a second?"

Rosie stared at her. "Is something wrong?"

"I think I've made a massive mistake."

"Tell me," Rosie said, feeling her stomach lurch. It could only be one thing.

"This morning... about an hour ago... I saw you cycling out of the yard so fast you nearly got hit by a car. I was worried about you," Jess started. "You just haven't seemed yourself lately."

"Go on," Rosie said.

"So I followed you... to South Grange."

"Oh no," Rosie said. "So you know about Jake,

then?" She paused. "Look, Jess, I felt really bad keeping it all a secret. I'm glad it's out in the open."

"I saw you crying, Rosie, and I recognized that boy. Did he hurt you?"

"No! He's my friend. I was upset about the cross-country team, that's all, and he was comforting me. Look, let me explain."

"I think it might be too late for explanations. I've done something really bad," Jess interrupted.

Rosie looked panicked. "You haven't told Nick have you?"

"Worse than that."

"*Worse?*" Rosie repeated. She looked at her friend's guilty face. "Please tell me you haven't called O'Grady?"

Jess nodded tearfully. "Rosie, I'm so sorry. I didn't mean to drop you in it."

"It's not me I'm worried about – it's Jake," said Rosie. "He stole Silver Dancer because O'Grady is planning to dope her. We *have* to warn him before it's too late. Come on, Jess!"

Chapter 12

Back to Sandy Lane...

"O'Grady will be on his way to Jake right now. But Elmwood is on the other side of Ash Hill, so we could still get to Jake and Dancer in time if we get a move on," Rosie shouted, racing down the drive on her bike.

"I'm right behind you!" Jess cried, zooming out of the yard. "I'm so, so sorry," she added, breathlessly, as they cycled along.

"It's not your fault," Rosie panted. "I shouldn't have kept it a secret from you. But where can Jake go now? He only had to stay hidden till tomorrow."

"Couldn't he come back to Sandy Lane?" Jess said. "He could tell Nick. I think we need some help in this."

"I hadn't wanted to drag the stables into it, but it's probably the only thing we can do now," Rosie said. "But O'Grady will come looking for you at Sandy Lane if Jake's not at South Grange, won't he?"

"He doesn't even know who I was, or that I was calling from Sandy Lane," Jess said. "He didn't give me a chance to tell him, horrible man."

Jake was clearly alarmed as soon as they pulled up in the yard.

"What are you doing here? I thought I'd told you to stay away, Rosie. And what's she doing here?" he said, pointing at Jess.

"No time for explanations," Rosie said. "We've got to go. O'Grady's on his way."

"What? How is O'Grady on his way? *Why?* Who told him we were here? I had all this worked out."

"It will be fine," Rosie said. "I've thought it all through. But you need to come on, Jake. We have to get out of here. I can explain everything later."

With a shrug, Jake quickly tacked up Silver Dancer and then followed Rosie and Jess on their cycles onto the road.

"Tell me where we're going and what this plan is, right now," he said.

"Well, as you only need to stay hidden for one more day, we thought it best if you came to our riding stables," Rosie explained.

"No way," Jake said, angrily. "Even more people will know about us. And hasn't O'Grady been to your stables before? Hasn't he met the owner?"

"Yes," Rosie said hesitantly. "He did come to talk to Nick, but that was before we knew the truth. If you explain things the way you did to me, I know Nick will help."

Jake looked unsure.

"You don't know him," Rosie went on. "I know he'll listen. He's very fair."

"He is," Jess added.

"Seems like you've decided for me."

"To be honest, I don't think you've got many options," said Rosie. "I know you wanted as few people involved as possible but the circumstances have changed. Do you want our help, or not?"

"I'm sorry," Jake said. "It's just a bit of a shock. And what do you mean, *the circumstances have changed*? I know you've done a lot for me, but—"

"Then let us do some more for you," Rosie said, cutting him off. "Look, we'll take the back way into Sandy Lane, through the trees, so no passing cars will spot us.

Jess and Rosie rode their bikes ahead of Jake and Silver Dancer into the thick woods. Once they were under the cover of the trees, everyone relaxed a little.

"But how *did* O'Grady find out?" Jake said. "And how did you know he was coming?"

Jess blushed. Rosie looked at her friend, sensing her discomfort.

"You could say it's my fault for keeping secrets from friends," she said. "But I'll explain more later.

We can't stop and talk, we should speed up. It's only another ten minutes, but the sooner we get there the better."

Pedalling on beside Jess, Rosie began to wonder what Nick would say. And what about the others? What would they say to her? Once the full story was out, they would realize that she'd been lying to them too. Rosie's head was pounding as she came to a halt at the gate on the other side of the woods.

"Right," she said. "Sandy Lane is just over there." She pointed across the fields. "Nick will be in a cross-country session around the back, so we can get into the yard without being seen. That way you can box Silver Dancer up and then we can tell Nick everything before he even knows she's there."

"Okay," Jake answered. "If you're sure that's the best way to play things."

Rosie nodded. "I am," she said. They crossed the coastal track and opened the gate to the back fields.

"Strange," Rosie murmured to Jess. "It sounds very quiet ahead of us. I'd have thought we'd be able to hear some sounds from the cross-country course."

"You're right. Perhaps they've stopped for a moment to listen to Nick give instructions."

Rosie jumped off her bike and opened the gate to the orchard. "Through here, Jake," she said.

Now that they had slowed their pace to a walk, Jake jumped down from Silver Dancer and led her by the reins.

Rosie was starting to feel better. Once they were at the yard, that beautiful horse would be out of harm's way.

"We're here," she said, opening the back gate.

"I'll take your bike and you lead her through," Jake suggested.

"Great," Rosie agreed and, grabbing Silver Dancer's reins, she led the way around the corner, followed by Jake. Jess brought up the rear. Suddenly, Rosie drew to an abrupt halt and gasped.

The yard was packed. Everyone was there and the usual chaos of the stables was well underway. The cross-country training must have ended sooner than they'd expected, Rosie realized with a sinking heart. There was nowhere to hide.

She tried to push Jake the way they'd just come but it was too late. Silver Dancer snorted loudly and tossed her mane. Everyone in the yard looked up, including Nick, who had an incredulous expression on his face.

"What on earth is going on?"

Chapter 13

The Secret Is Out

The yard was completely silent for several long seconds. Even the horses seemed to be staring at Jake, Rosie, Jess and Silver Dancer. Nick stood with his mouth wide open, his expression a mixture of surprise and shock. Finally, Rosie managed to say something to break the awkward silence.

"Nick, this is Silver Dancer and Jake Goodman," she said, her voice squeaking with nerves.

"Well, I think I'd worked that out, thank you," Nick answered coldly. "How many racehorses do we get turning up around here? I thought I could trust you and Jess! Now, the three of you had better explain yourselves and then I'll call Elmwood Racing Stables."

"NO!" Jake burst out. "No, please don't call the stables whatever you do."

Nick's stern look silenced him before he could say anything else.

"We know it looks bad, but Rosie only wanted to help Silver Dancer," Jess said. "She didn't even tell me what's been going on."

"Oh really," Nick snapped, seeming to grow more irritated by the second.

"Look," Jake said, stepping forward. "It isn't Rosie's fault. I dragged her into all this. I know it looks pretty bad, and I wouldn't have bothered you if I had a choice. But Jess and Rosie said you'd listen. They said you were fair..."

Nick ran his fingers through his hair, suddenly looking weary.

"Come on, Nick." Sarah, his wife, appeared behind him. "I agree it doesn't look good, but let's hear what the boy has to say before we just hand him over to O'Grady."

"Hmm... We'll go inside and talk first, then," Nick said, a little more kindly.

Jake tied up Silver Dancer and followed Nick. Rosie and Jess went to go after them, but Nick shook his head.

"Uh uh. If you two want to be useful, go and get that horse fed and watered. Put her in the end stable. Can I trust you to manage that?"

"Yes, Nick," said Rosie, anxious to help but desperately wanting to see how things would go. All she could do was watch as Jake disappeared with Nick and Sarah into the cottage.

A few minutes later, Silver Dancer was happily munching a haynet in her box. Rosie and Jess felt they had to go over to the cottage, ignoring the questions from the other riders in the yard. The others would have to wait for answers.

The next twenty minutes seemed endless, as both girls sat on the step outside the cottage waiting, until Jake finally came out.

"It's all right," he said. "He's agreed to help."

Nick appeared behind him. "Jake's going to stay here for the night in the room above the barn. But he's made a very serious allegation and I need to speak to Josh first thing tomorrow when he's back. Now, I want you to go home – and no mention of this to anyone yet. Is that understood?"

He looked around at the other riders, who had wandered over as they saw the cottage door open.

Everyone nodded and started to leave the stables to go home – all except Rosie and Jess.

"And you two," Nick said. "Try and get a good night's sleep. I'll see you both back here tomorrow, when I hope we'll get to the bottom of this."

Chapter 14

Confrontation

"Hello, is that Josh? It's Nick Brooks here, from Sandy Lane."

Rosie thought how business-like Nick sounded, as she tried to listen in to his conversation. She had come to the stables early and she could see Jake sitting at the desk in the office, biting his nails. He must be nervous too. She wished Jess were here, but she'd had a dentist's appointment.

"Yes, I heard that your horse had been taken, Josh. That's why I'm phoning," Nick said. "I've got some information on her whereabouts. It's a little delicate to be honest. Do you think you could come over here as soon as possible and on your own? Great, thanks for your understanding."

He put the phone down and smiled at Jake. "He's coming straight over."

"How did he sound?" Jake asked anxiously.

"Concerned, and a bit suspicious of me, but I think he'll listen to reason. He's a good man."

"Yeah I know," Jake said. "I'm just worried that O'Grady might have got to him already. He's been his head lad for some time now."

"You can only do your best, Jake... Just tell him your side of things."

"If you don't mind, I think I'll go and groom Dancer now," replied Jake. "I don't want him to think I haven't been caring for her properly."

"Sure." Nick nodded and Jake slipped out of the tack room.

Rosie looked up at Nick. "Do you believe him?" she asked.

"Yes, I think I do. I know what goes on in racing

circles where there's a lot of money and reputations at stake. It's a whole world away from a riding stables like this."

Rosie saw a familiar wistful look in his eyes and knew that Nick was remembering his days as a successful National Hunt jockey. He had given it up to set up Sandy Lane and loved his job. What he had never given up was his love of the racing world too.

"Seeing his earnestness, I couldn't help myself trusting him," Nick went on. "Just a gut reaction. He's young, this is his first job and he obviously loves horses. I don't think he'd have risked everything for no good reason. But it's up to Josh to sort it now. I can't really do much more – and it's not really our business anyway."

Rosie started as she heard a Land Rover pull up in the yard.

"That'll be Josh," said Nick. "I'd better go and meet him."

Rosie watched as a tall man stepped out of the car. When he saw Jake, his face darkened.

"You've got a nerve, just standing there as if nothing's happened. Where is she? What have you done with her?" he demanded.

"She's all right," Nick interrupted, leading the way across the yard to where Silver Dancer had been stabled. "See for yourself – she's in good form." He opened the door and Josh went forward and ran a hand down her legs.

"Hmm... She seems fit and healthy enough," he said begrudgingly.

Jake stood in the doorway, saying nothing.

"She's all ready to go back to Elmwood with you, but I really think you need to hear what this boy has to say before you take her," said Nick.

Josh turned on Jake, his face flushed with anger. "What did you think you were doing taking her when her race was only a week away? You could have ruined everything. Thank goodness O'Grady hasn't cancelled her entry."

"I think it might be best if we all go and sit down," Nick said. "Can you get a box sent over for her?"

Josh nodded and the three of them walked into the tack room. Rosie stood outside, desperately wanting to join in and say something in Jake's defence, but this was something he had to tackle on his own. He had taken all the decisions.

"I'm all ears," she heard Josh say, in a kinder voice. No one noticed Rosie, hovering just outside the door, hoping he really would listen to Jake.

Jake looked across at Nick for reassurance and Nick nodded.

"Well..." Jake said. "To start with, whatever O'Grady's been saying about me or the stables, it's not true."

Josh folded his arms. "Go on."

"You see, odd things have been going on at the yard," said Jake, nervously. "There were these strange men who used to appear whenever you weren't around, but when I asked O'Grady about them, he'd just tell me to keep my nose out."

"Nothing odd about that. They're probably old friends of his," said Josh defensively.

"But then there were all these phone calls I overheard as well," Jake went on. "I heard O'Grady talking about doping Silver Dancer before her race. He mentioned a huge sum of money, so I think he's desperate. There wasn't anyone I could talk to, Josh, because you were away, so the only thing I could think to do was to take her away and keep her safe."

Jake's words had speeded up in his anxiety to explain everything. Now he stopped, his fists clenched as he waited to hear what Josh had to say.

"Do you believe all this?" Josh asked Nick, thoughtfully.

"Yes, yes I think I do," Nick said.

Josh turned back to Jake. "But why should I believe you, Jake? O'Grady's been with me for fifteen years. He's told me about all the trouble you've been causing with the other boys at the yard, and that you're lazy, too. Oh, and about your attitude when he didn't give you the rides you wanted. I have to say, it doesn't sound good."

"It wasn't like that!" Jake cried out, looking to

Nick for help, but Nick couldn't offer any. This was Josh's territory.

"I had high hopes for you, Jake," Josh went on, "but I'm going to have to let you go."

Jake gripped the table so hard that Rosie saw his knuckles turn white. He shook his head, tears forming in his eyes that he angrily blinked away.

"Nick, thanks for calling me. I can see why you listened to him... really I can," Josh said sadly. "But what can I do? I have to go with my head lad."

Nick nodded gravely. "I understand."

"Look Jake, I believe you meant well, and I'm not a man to hold grudges. If you go away quietly, I won't involve the police."

He took out his phone and rang a number. "Hello... Yes it's me. I've got Silver Dancer here, so I need a box. Yes, yes she's all right. We're at Sandy Lane Stables, near Ash Hill. Cheers."

Jake stood up. "I won't let you. I won't let you take her. I haven't gone through all this for her to be in danger again," he said, fiercely.

Rosie felt dreadful. She was so sorry for him but on hearing Jake's passionate outburst, Josh's face had simply hardened.

Nick laid his hand on Jake's arm. "Cool down, Jake. I am sorry about all this but Silver Dancer is Josh's horse. You can't stop him from taking her."

Jake gulped and nodded. He was beaten and he knew it.

"Come and collect your things while O'Grady and I are on the gallops tomorrow, Jake," Josh said. "We'll be busy trying to get Silver Dancer ready for Monday's race. Could be difficult, as she's lost a week's training already..."

Jake walked out of the tack room, his shoulders slumped with despair. Rosie could see he was heartbroken and she felt as if she were, too...

Chapter 15

A Plan Is Hatched

Rosie stood by Jake's side as they watched Silver Dancer being led into the box and driven off back to Elmwood. There was nothing more he could do, but she had seen how much it had hurt him when Josh had not believed him.

Nick joined them, seeing a look of burning fury flash across Jake's face. "I know you thought you were doing the right thing," he said quietly. "But you were probably worrying unnecessarily. Josh would know if there was any sort of problem at his stables. Look, I can tell you're good with horses, so you're welcome to stay here with us till you find your feet, if you like."

"Thanks, but... I can't afford to pay you," Jake said, embarrassed.

"No problem," said Nick. "Help us around the yard, that'll be payment enough."

"Thanks, Nick," Jake said.

"Right, back to work. See you two later." As Nick strode off towards the outdoor school, Jake turned to Rosie.

"Nick's great, but it doesn't change the fact that Josh didn't believe me, does it? So that means it was all for nothing."

"You're safe and Silver Dancer's safe, Jake, whatever you say," Rosie replied, trying to comfort him. "O'Grady's not going to dare do anything after what you've just told Josh."

"Don't bet on it," Jake said, getting more worked up. "You didn't hear how desperate he was in that last phone call. I did. And if she doesn't run well, he can just blame me – say she wasn't fit enough, because I made her miss vital training days."

"But that wouldn't be true," said Rosie indignantly. "You were training her every day."

"What's going on?" A breathless Jess pedalled into the yard. "I saw a horse box pulling out. What's happened? Where's Silver Dancer?"

"Dancer's gone," Rosie answered, telling Jess the whole story.

When she had finished, Jess was outraged. "I can't believe it! So what are you going to do now, Jake?" she asked.

"There's not a lot I can do, is there?" he said, sounding weary and utterly defeated.

"You mean you're giving in?"

"He's just being realistic, Jess," said Rosie.

"I don't believe you two." Jess looked furious. "What a pair of wimps! And I can't believe Nick just let them take her away."

"He couldn't stop them, could he, Jess," Rosie said, her voice bitter with her own disappointment. "Silver Dancer isn't his horse."

"And O'Grady has been clever. He came up with all sorts of lies about me. Josh thinks the worst. Who knows what O'Grady told Nick when he first came here," Jake added.

"But if Silver Dancer's racing on Monday, O'Grady's still got time to strike," cried Jess. "Do you want that possibility hanging over your heads? You can't give up now. We'll just have to go over there and keep watch on her."

Jake looked thoughtful. "Jess is right. O'Grady can't do anything during the day, there are too many people about, but at night, he still could." He paused. "I'll keep watch then, starting tonight," he decided, a determined look on his face.

"We're all in it together," Jess said, her eyes shining with excitement. "I came up with this idea, and, besides, you look exhausted. What happens if you fall asleep?"

"Good point," said Rosie.

"Okay then, but you do know this could turn nasty, don't you? Even dangerous. O'Grady's not going to give in without a fight."

Rosie and Jess nodded. They understood that there were risks.

"Maybe we should keep out of each other's way this afternoon," Jake suggested. "Nick might realize we're up to something if we hang around together and I don't think he'd be pleased."

"Where and when shall we meet up tonight?" Rosie asked.

"Seven o'clock," Jake said firmly. He seemed relieved to be doing something, rather than just waiting for things to happen. "At the bus stop by the corner of Sandy Lane. We can get the bus to Elmwood together. Okay?"

Jess and Rosie both nodded.

"Good. We have a plan," Jake said.

Chapter 16

Keeping Watch

Rosie stood at the corner of Sandy Lane, stamping her feet to keep them warm. It was a cold night and it had just started to rain: not ideal for their first night's outing. She looked at her phone. It was seven o'clock already. Where were the others? The bus would be here any minute...

She sighed as she thought of all the lies she'd had to tell to be here at all. She'd pretended to be ill and gone to bed early, then stuffed some pillows under her duvet and climbed out of her bedroom window. She really hoped her mum wouldn't find out. Rosie felt guilty enough already and her mum would be beside herself with worry if she found Rosie missing.

Jake was the next to arrive. "Sorry I'm late," he muttered. "Nick was in the yard."

"He didn't see you leaving, did he?"

"Don't think so."

"That's a relief," said Rosie.

"You know, I'm sure O'Grady will try something tonight. Silver Dancer's racing on Monday. He can't risk leaving it much later."

Rosie agreed, and then saw Jess sprinting up the road towards them.

"I thought I was never going to get away," Jess said, panting heavily. "Mum and Dad are out, so I had to get past my brother. I waited until he was calling his girlfriend, then sneaked out. With any luck, I'll be back before Mum and Dad get in and my brother won't even notice I'm gone."

The bus pulled up beside them and they got on and sat down in silence. Jake was very quiet the whole way, staring out of the window, and Rosie didn't like to disturb him. They hadn't discussed what they would do if they actually caught O'Grady red-handed, but Rosie knew they were all thinking about it. It seemed hours before the bus finally reached Elmwood.

"How on earth are we going to get in?" Rosie whispered, staring up at the huge iron gates of the racing stables.

"Follow me," Jake murmured. "I know a back way through the training gallops. I'm pretty sure they'll have put Dancer in her usual box – third along from the tack room. We'll get a clear view from the back."

They crept through the trees and across the moonlit grass. The only sound was the occasional hoot from an owl.

"Josh lives over there." Jake pointed to an elegant house behind the stable yard.

"At least he won't be able to see us from that far away," Jess muttered.

"But that won't stop O'Grady," Jake said. "He lives in one of the annexes above the stables, so we'll have to be very careful he doesn't catch us."

Rosie shivered. She had only met the man once, but she'd heard so much about him now that she was starting to feel frightened. This was such a serious business and they were trespassing too. Only the thought of Silver Dancer kept her going.

"Right," said Jake, "around this corner, then we're going to have to go one by one over to the barn."

"Jake!" Rosie grabbed his arm in panic. "You mean we have to cross the yard?"

"I know it looks a long way," Jake said. "But they'll have done their nightly checks of the stables by now. No one will be about. I'll go first and I'll wave at you once I'm there."

"But... but what if we get caught?" Rosie asked.

"We'll just have to make sure we don't," said Jake, with a determined grin. He stepped out of the shadows and began to walk across the gravel. Rosie jumped as his footsteps crunched in the darkness, but no one appeared.

"Me next," Jess said firmly. Rosie watched Jess

disappear across the yard and into the barn. Rosie's heart was pounding as she hurried across the gravel to join them.

"Now, we wait," Jake whispered.

"It's freezing," Rosie said. She sat down in the hay, glad that at least one part of their dangerous adventure was over. Jess could not sit still and jigged about with nervous excitement.

"Sit down, Jess, please," Jake said, crossly. "You keep making me think I can hear someone coming."

Jess went over to join Rosie, but within minutes she was looking out of the back window again. She was obviously scared and her nerves were affecting Jake, who was getting more jittery by the minute.

By eight o'clock, Rosie was convinced that O'Grady wouldn't do anything now that Josh's suspicions were aroused. She was sure that their efforts were a waste of time.

Jake walked over to the entrance of the barn and looked out.

"This was not one of my better ideas," Jess hissed

to Rosie. "We've been here for ages, and nothing... The more I think about it, the less likely—"

"Sshh!" Jake waved at them. He'd heard something. The girls crept over to join him just as the beam from a flashlight rested on the barn for a moment. They all sprang back into the darkness and crouched down, holding their breath.

When the beam moved away, Rosie slowly climbed up and peered out of the window... to catch a glimpse of the person holding the flashlight: O'Grady.

"It's him," Rosie hissed.

"Didn't you say Silver Dancer's stable was the third one along?" Jess whispered to Jake.

Jake nodded grimly. It was only a matter of time. All they could hear was the crunch of shoes on gravel as the flashlight flickered around the yard. Rosie kept watching, her heart pounding as if she had run all the way there. O'Grady was disappearing into Silver Dancer's stable.

Rosie felt faint. They hadn't planned what they

were going to do when what was happening actually happened. She looked at Jake, wondering if he was thinking the same thing, when she saw him start. There was another figure in the yard. An accomplice? No, she saw with relief. It was Josh Wiley. He was moving stealthily towards the same stable. Silently, Rosie watched him as he edged closer to the door, and then seemed to stop and listen outside. Suddenly, Josh's deep voice boomed out: "What on earth are you doing?"

O'Grady had clearly been taken by surprise, because he wasn't able to reply beyond spluttering noises. Rosie found herself wishing she could see his face.

"What are you doing in Silver Dancer's stable at this time of night?" Josh shouted. "And what's in your hand? That's going in her food, I suppose?"

There were the sounds of a scuffle and then all was quiet.

Jake, Rosie and Jess stayed completely still, as Josh's voice rang out again.

"I trusted you, O'Grady," Josh said. "We've worked together for so long." Rosie could hear real sadness in his voice now, instead of white fury.

"It was only going to be the once, Josh, honestly – please believe me," O'Grady pleaded. "I needed the money. I'm in so much debt..."

"Who's paying you to do this?" Josh asked.

Jake's face was solemn and pale. This was important.

"Come on," Jess said, nudging him. "You want to know who's to blame for all this, too. Go out there and confront him."

"I don't think you should, Jake," said Rosie. "Now isn't the time."

"No," Jake agreed. "It isn't. O'Grady has been caught out and Silver Dancer will be safe now. It's up to Josh to sort it out from here."

"But—" Jess started.

"No buts," said Jake, firmly.

"Well, if that's what you want," said Jess, with a shrug. "It's not what I'd do..." And then she smiled to show there were no hard feelings.

When Rosie looked back into the yard, the two figures had disappeared and the place was empty.

"They've probably gone inside to talk," Jake said. "I think we ought to head home, too. I'd like to check on Silver Dancer, but if we're caught, we'll be in big trouble. I'm sure it won't be long before we hear more about it. Everything will be all right now Josh is on the case, you'll see."

Chapter 17

Back at the Yard

To their great relief, both Rosie and Jess got home without anyone realizing they had been out and they decided not even to tell Nick about what they'd done that night. Things would come out into the open soon enough.

When the two girls arrived at Sandy Lane the next morning, they were surprised to see Nick and Jake talking in the tack room.

Rosie left Jess with Skylark and, rushing over, stuck her head around the door. Surely Jake wasn't telling Nick when they had agreed not to?

"Oh hello," Nick smiled at Rosie. "I was just showing Jake the feed rotas."

"Oh, right," said Rosie, feeling relieved and going back to tell Jess. Their secret was still safe.

"It looks as if Nick's about to find out anyway," Jess added, as a Land Rover pulled up in the drive and Josh stepped out.

"Oh, er, hi Josh," Nick said, looking surprised and sounding slightly embarrassed. "I hope you don't mind, but I said Jake could stay here for a few days. I could do with the help, to be honest."

"No problem. I thought you might help him out," Josh said. "You've done me a favour, in fact."

Josh started to tell them what had happened the night before in Silver Dancer's stable. Rosie, Jess and Jake tried to show shock and surprise in all the right places, which wasn't easy.

"I really wanted to believe you, Jake, because I thought deep down you were a good lad," Josh explained, "but I felt I had to give O'Grady the benefit of the doubt. Then, when I got back to the yard, things just didn't add up. He'd gone on and on about all the trouble you'd caused, but when I checked with the other lads at the stables, no one agreed with him. So I decided to watch him, and you were right, he was up to something – but this mess goes further than that. He was actually working for someone else. O'Grady's not the puppet-master in all this. He's just the puppet."

Jake shrugged his shoulders, as if he'd guessed that anyway. Rosie decided that it must be hard to forgive someone for not trusting you.

"It was all so pointless too," Josh said gloomily. "If only O'Grady had come to me and told me he was having financial troubles, I'd have helped, but the thought of easy money was too much for him. And now I know the man behind it all. It was Brad Thompson, a trainer on the other side of Walbrook. He had two horses in Silver Dancer's race. He's already being investigated by the Jockey Club for corruption. With O'Grady's testimony, he should lose his licence. He could even go to prison."

"And has O'Grady agreed to stand up in court?" asked Jake.

"Well he couldn't exactly refuse," Josh answered. "I told him I wouldn't press charges if he did. I can't have him back at Elmwood, though, so he'll lose his home and his job, but I'd be glad to save him from prison. Fifteen years he's been with me... It's a long time." He shook his head sadly.

"Thanks for coming over and sorting things out so quickly," said Nick. "It must have been terrible for you, the whole business."

"I can't tell you how sorry I am about all of it," Josh went on. "And I do want to clear the air, if I can." He turned to Jake. "Your old job is still there for you. If you want it, that is."

"Really? If I want it?" Jake cried. "Of course I want it!"

Josh laughed. "I do need to ask you a favour, though. A big favour. It's about Silver Dancer and her race tomorrow," he began. "You see, O'Grady hasn't booked a jockey."

Rosie saw Jake's face light up. Both of them knew what was coming.

"I know it's short notice, but I was wondering if you would ride her."

"Ride her? In her big race... in the Latchfield?" Jake's eyes widened.

"Well, I don't think she's down to race in any other." Josh laughed. "I've seen you go together on the gallops, so I know you can do it, and the horse knows you. Look, you don't have to give me an answer right now, you can think about it. I will need to know by this evening though."

"I don't need to wait till this evening," Jake said, beaming from ear to ear. "I'd love to ride her... if you're sure."

"I'm sure," Josh said.

"This is so awesome, Jake," said Rosie, wondering whether she should give him a hug or not. She and Jess were almost as excited as he was.

"Right, well, if it's okay with you, Jake, we'd better get back to Elmwood," Josh said. "There's still a lot of work to be done for you to be ready to ride Silver Dancer tomorrow.

Jake grinned. "I'll just get my things."

"So I guess this means I'll be losing my new stable hand then," Nick broke in, smiling.

"Oh, I-I-" Jake stuttered.

Rosie and Jess smiled at each other. They knew when Nick was teasing.

"Go on." Nick laughed. "I'm only joking, Jake! Of course you must go."

Jake didn't need to be told twice. He started to run over to his room above the barn when he stopped and walked back to Rosie.

"I don't know what to say," he said.

"Don't say anything," Rosie replied. "Just get to Elmwood and get practising." She smiled. "You've got a race to win."

Ten minutes later, they all watched as the car drove away, Jake's arm waving wildly out of his window until they were out of sight.

"Well..." Rosie sighed. "That's all very exciting,

but it's back to school tomorrow, worst luck. We won't even be able to watch the race."

"Don't worry." Nick grinned. "I'll be sure to record it for you, then you can watch it as many times as you like."

"Great!" cried Rosie and Jess in unison.

"You'd better make the most of your last day of half-term," said Nick. "And now all the drama with Silver Dancer is finished, haven't you two got something to do? We're supposed to be going out over the cross-country course in ten minutes."

Rosie's face fell. She had almost forgotten that she was not in the team.

"Oh Rosie," Nick began, seeing her glum expression. "Look, I know you're disappointed you aren't in the Roxburgh team, and I can't change that, but Izzy's not going to be able to come to many of the competitions after this one. So, if you've got time in your frantic schedule to fit in the practices, you never know, you might get your old place back after all." He winked.

"Of course I've got time for the practices!" Rosie laughed, her confidence starting to return.

She turned to Jess and smiled. "In fact, there's nowhere in the world I'd rather be."

With that, the two girls headed over to the stables to tack up their horses, ready for another wonderful morning of riding.

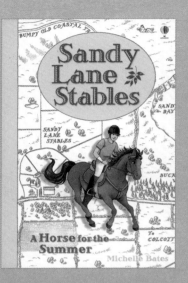

A Horse for the Summer

Michelle Bates

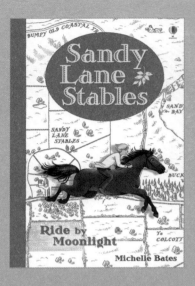

Ride by Moonlight

Michelle Bates

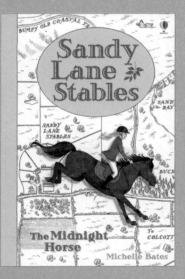

The Midnight Horse

Michelle Bates

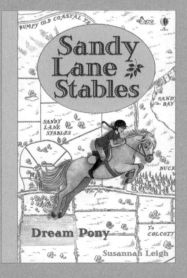

Dream Pony

Susannah Leigh